A Fresh-n-Fruity Spring

By Lauren Cecil
Illustrated by MJ Illustrations

Grosset & Dunlap
An Imprint of Penguin Group (USA) Inc.

GROSSET & DUNLAP
Published by the Penguin Group
Penguin Group (USA) Inc., 375 Hudson Street,
New York, New York 10014, USA
Penguin Group (Canada), 90 Eglinton Avenue East, Suite 700,
Toronto, Ontario M4P 2Y3, Canada
(a division of Pearson Penguin Canada Inc.)
Penguin Books Ltd., 80 Strand, London WC2R 0RL, England
Penguin Group Ireland, 25 St. Stephen's Green, Dublin 2, Ireland
(a division of Penguin Books Ltd.)
Penguin Group (Australia), 250 Camberwell Road, Camberwell, Victoria 3124, Australia
(a division of Pearson Australia Group Pty. Ltd.)
Penguin Books India Pvt. Ltd., 11 Community Centre,
Panchsheel Park, New Delhi—110 017, India
Penguin Group (NZ), 67 Apollo Drive, Rosedale, North Shore 0632, New Zealand
(a division of Pearson New Zealand Ltd.)
Penguin Books (South Africa) (Pty.) Ltd., 24 Sturdee Avenue,
Rosebank, Johannesburg 2196, South Africa

Penguin Books Ltd., Registered Offices:
80 Strand, London WC2R 0RL, England

Library of Congress Control Number: 2009017822

ISBN 978-0-448-45273-9   10 9 8

It was a perfect day for a walk in Berry Bitty City. The sun was shining. Birds were singing. And flowers were blooming everywhere.
"What a berry nice day!" Strawberry Shortcake said to Orange Blossom.

"Isn't this weather beautiful?" Blueberry Muffin called to her friends as they passed her bookshop.

"And do you know what beautiful weather means?" asked Strawberry.

"SPRING!" they all cheered at once.

"What do you think is the best thing about spring?"
Orange asked her friends.
"The flowers!" said Strawberry.
"The delicious fruit!" said Blueberry.

"I've got a great idea!" Orange suddenly cried.

"What is it?" Strawberry asked.

"I can't explain now!" said Orange as she headed for home. "See you later!"

Strawberry and Blueberry were very confused. What could Orange's idea be?

The next day, Strawberry and Blueberry went to Orange's
store. They saw a new sign hanging in the window.
    "Special Spring Gifts Inside," Strawberry read aloud.
    "Hmm . . ." said Blueberry. "Let's go see what she's up to!"

"Is this your great idea?" asked Blueberry.
"Yes! I'm making bunches of flowers and yummy fruit baskets to celebrate spring," Orange explained.

"What a berry good idea!" said Strawberry. "I'd like to order flowers for my café."

"And I'd like a fruit basket for my bookstore," said Blueberry.

"Great!" replied Orange. "I'll deliver them tomorrow morning."

The next day, Orange stopped by Strawberry's café.

"Hi, Strawberry!" Orange called cheerfully. "I have the flowers you ordered."

"Oh, Orange! They're so pretty," said Strawberry. "I'll put them on the counter. Thank you!"

Next, Orange visited Blueberry's bookstore.

"Hello, Blueberry!" Orange greeted her friend. "I have your fruit basket."

"Wow!" said Blueberry. "This looks great. I'm going to set it right here. Now all my customers can have a taste. Thanks, Orange!"

Later that day, Raspberry Torte and Lemon Meringue
dropped by Orange's store.

"Lemon and I would like to order flowers," said Raspberry.

"No problem," said Orange. "I'll deliver them both tomorrow."

"Thanks!" the girls called as they left the store.

Just after Raspberry and Lemon left, Orange's phone rang. "Hi, Orange. It's Plum Pudding. I'd like to order a fruit basket," Plum said.

"Sure thing," replied Orange. "I'll drop it off tomorrow." "Thanks!" said Plum.

All day long, the word spread about Orange's special spring gifts.
Soon there was a line of customers outside Orange's door.

14

"Wow, Orange. You're really busy!" Strawberry said.
"I know," said Orange. "I can't believe how many orders I have!"
"Do you need any help?" Blueberry offered.
"No, I can do it all myself," Orange said. "But thanks!"

The next day, Orange zoomed around Berry Bitty City delivering her orders. She was in such a rush. She couldn't even stop to say hello to her friends.

First, Orange dropped off a package at Raspberry's shop. When Raspberry opened it, she saw a fruit basket. "But I ordered flowers!" said Raspberry.

Then Orange dropped off a package at Plum's dance studio. When Plum opened it, she found flowers.
"But I ordered a fruit basket!" said Plum.

Next, Orange dropped off Lemon's package.
When Lemon opened it, she found a very strange bouquet.
It was filled with fruit <u>and</u> flowers.
"This is definitely not what I ordered!" Lemon cried.

The girls went back to Orange's store to return their fruit and flowers.

"Our orders are all mixed up," explained Raspberry. "I got fruit instead of flowers."

"And I got flowers instead of fruit," added Plum.

"And I don't even know what I got," said Lemon.

"I am so sorry," Orange gasped. "I can't seem to keep track of all my orders!"

"Maybe we could help you," Raspberry offered.

"No, that's okay," insisted Orange. "I can handle it myself."

The next day, Orange's friends met up at Strawberry's café. They were worried about Orange.

"Orange has too many spring orders," Raspberry said. "She needs our help."

"But how can we help her when she won't let us?" asked Blueberry.

"I have an idea!" Strawberry said. "Let's all go to Orange's store this afternoon."

Later, all the girls rode their scooters to Orange's store.
"What are you doing here?" Orange asked her friends.
"We're here to help with your spring deliveries!" said Strawberry.

"You don't have to do that," Orange insisted.
"But that's what friends are for," said Strawberry.
"It's okay to ask for help sometimes."

Orange looked around her store. It was a mess!
She could not do everything on her own.
   "You're right," said Orange. "Thank you! Now let's
get these packages delivered!"

Each girl loaded up her scooter. Then they drove off in different directions.

Finally, all the packages were delivered.
"Thanks for your help," Orange said to her
friends. "I couldn't have done it without you!"

"You're welcome, Orange," Strawberry said. "But there is one delivery we forgot to make."

"Oh no!" Orange cried. "Whose delivery did we forget?"

"Yours!" Strawberry cried as she held out
a dazzling bunch of flowers.

"While we were making deliveries, we each picked the prettiest flowers we could find. Then we made an extra special bouquet for you!" said Strawberry.

"Thank you!" Orange said. "You are the best!
And this is going to be the most wonderful spring ever!"